Earth Friends at the Grocery Store

Francine Galko

Heinemann Library
Chicago, Illinois

Customer Service   888–454–2279

Visit our website at www.heinemannlibrary.com

Designed by Anna Matras/Heinemann Library
Illustration by Carrie Gowran
Photo research by Heather Sabel
Printed and bound in Hong Kong and China
by South China Printing Company Limited

08 07 06 05 04
10 9 8 7 6 5 4 3 2 1

**Library of Congress
Cataloging-in-Publication Data**
Galko, Francine.
  Earth friends at the grocery store / Francine Galko.
  p. cm. -- (Earth friends)
  Summary: Discusses the importance of reducing
waste, recycling, and reusing products in the context
of grocery shopping.
  Includes bibliographical references and index.
  ISBN 1-4034-4898-1 (library binding-hardcover) --
  ISBN 1-4034-4903-1 (pbk.)
  1. Environmental protection--Citizen participation--
Juvenile literature. 2. Grocery shopping--Juvenile
literature. 3. Recycling (Waste, etc.)--Juvenile
literature. [1. Environmental protection--Citizen
participation. 2. Grocery shopping. 3. Recycling
(Waste)] I. Title. TD171.7.G3523 2004
  363.72'8--dc2   2003021005

Acknowledgments
The author and publisher are grateful to the
following for permission to reproduce copyright
material: p. 4 Corbis; pp. 5, 6, 9, 11, 12, 13, 15,
16, 17, 19, 20, 23, 24, 25, 27, 28, 30 Robert
Lifson/Heinemann Library; pp. 8, 10, 14 Jill
Birschbach/Heinemann Library; p. 18 Angela
Hampton/Ecoscene/Corbis; p. 21 SW Production/
Index Stock Imagery; pp. 22, 26, 29 Greg
Williams/Heinemann Library

Cover photo by Robert Lifson/Heinemann Library

Some words are
shown in bold,
like this. You can
find out what they
mean by looking
in the glossary.

To learn about the picture on
the front cover, turn to page 9.

Contents

What Is an Earth Friend?

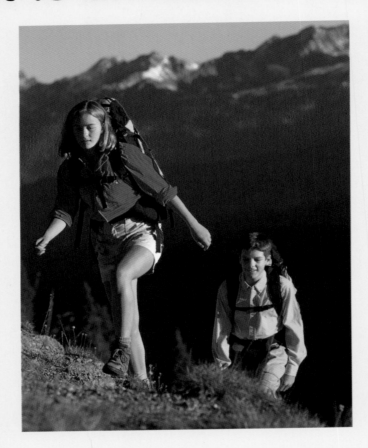

Earth friends use **natural resources** carefully. Natural resources are important **materials** found in nature. Air, water, land, and trees are natural resources.

These people are **reusing** cloth shopping bags.

Earth friends use only what they need.
They do not waste natural resources.
Earth friends also help keep Earth clean.

Reduce, Reuse, and Recycle

When you use **natural resources,** use as few as you can. Paper plates are made from trees. Do not use and throw away paper plates. Buy **sturdy plastic** plates that you can wash and **reuse.**

reusable plastic plate

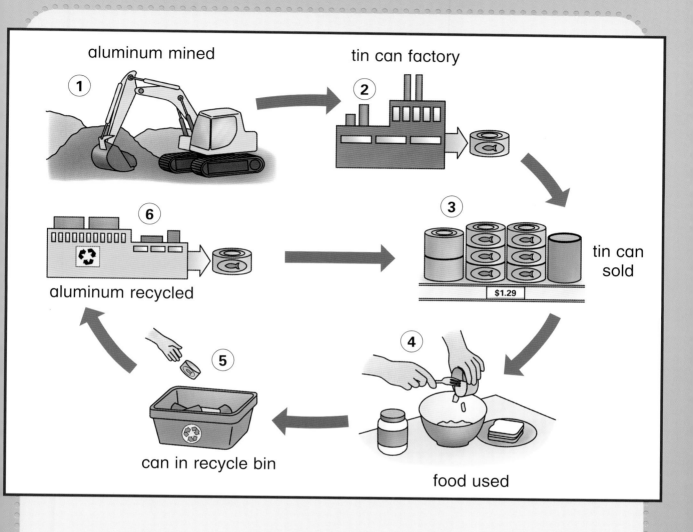

1. aluminum mined
2. tin can factory
3. tin can sold
4. food used
5. can in recycle bin
6. aluminum recycled

$1.29

Recycle things when you can. **Aluminum, tin,** glass, plastic, and paper can often be recycled. You can choose food in tin cans. Recycle the cans after you eat the food.

Bring Your Own Bags

Every time you buy something, you bring it home in a bag. Soon you have a lot of bags at home. If you throw them away, they take up space in a **landfill.**

When you go shopping, bring cloth or net bags that you can use again. Or bring **plastic** or paper bags from another shopping trip. **Reuse** bags when you can.

cloth
shopping bag

Buy Only What You Need

Before you go shopping, make a list of what you need. When you are at the store, you might see something that is not on your list. Ask yourself if you really need it.

Advertisements try to make people want to buy things. Think about the advertisements you see. Say no to advertisements for things that you do not need.

This toy is not on the girl's shopping list.

Buy Things That Last

People throw away **disposable** products quickly. For example, paper plates and paper towels are disposable. Disposable products fill up **landfills.** When you shop, choose things that will last a long time.

Do not buy paper towels. Buy cloth towels instead. You can wash them and **reuse** them again and again.

cloth towel

Send Less to the Landfill

regular lightbulb

long-lasting lightbulb

Some lightbulbs work much longer than others do. These lightbulbs cost more at the store. But they cost less to use. This **reduces** the number of lightbulbs that go to **landfills.**

When **batteries** stop working, they have lost their **charge.** People throw them away. But **rechargeable** batteries can be used again and again. They last longer than regular batteries.

Choose Safe Products

People use cleaners to clean up around the house. Many cleaners have strong **chemicals.** These chemicals harm us and Earth. Talk to your parents about buying safe, **nontoxic** cleaners for your house.

cleaner with chemicals

Some soaps, shampoos, and creams are made from **harmful** chemicals. Others are made from natural **ingredients**. They are better for your body and Earth.

Choose the Safest Foods

Farmers grow most of the food you see at the grocery store. Some farmers use **dangerous chemicals** that keep bugs from harming their crops. These chemicals can harm Earth and people.

Organic farmers grow foods without dangerous chemicals. Read the **labels** to find out which foods were grown without chemicals. Organic foods are better for you and Earth.

organic apple

Reduce Trash

Pay attention to **packages.** If you use juice boxes, all of the boxes and straws will go to a **landfill.** But a big **plastic** bottle of juice can be **recycled.**

Nine juice boxes hold as much juice as one big bottle like this one.

Some pet food comes in small cans so that
it stays fresh. But this makes a lot of trash.
You can buy pet food in large bags. Keep
it fresh in a **reusable container** at home.
This **reduces** the amount of garbage you make.

Buy Recyclable Packages

People throw away lot of **packages**. Then a garbage truck takes them to a **landfill**. Sometimes the trash is burned. The fewer things you throw away, the cleaner Earth will be.

Some packaging **materials** can be **recycled.**
Metal, glass, **plastic,** and **cardboard**
are often recycled. Try to buy recyclable
packages at the grocery store.

Paper milk cartons are not recyclable, but plastic milk jugs can be recycled.

Choose Earth-Friendly Packages

wrapped in plastic

not wrapped

Some fruits and vegetables come wrapped in **plastic** or plastic foam. These things cannot be **recycled.** They stay in **landfills** for a long, long time.

Some toothpaste comes in fancy pumps. Many of these pumps hold less toothpaste than a tube. Pumps also take up more space in landfills. Choose toothpaste in a tube.

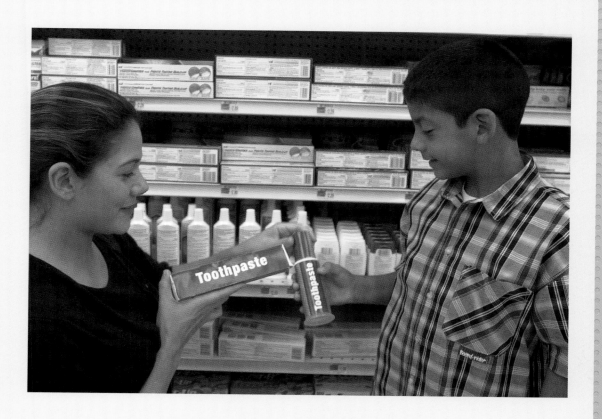

Recycle Plastic Containers

Plastic is used to make many different **containers.** Plastic comes from **coal** or oil. Plastic can be useful, but it cannot always be **recycled.**

recyclable

not recyclable

Some plastic containers can be recycled.
A number 1 or 2 on the package means
that it can be recycled in most places.
Choose plastic containers that you can recycle.

Buy Things Made from Recycled Materials

It is not enough to just **recycle.** You can also buy things made from recycled **materials.** Writing paper, toilet paper, and wrapping paper can be made from recycled paper.

recycled paper

Paper egg cartons are usually made from recycled paper.

Choose products in **aluminum**, glass, or gray **cardboard packages.** These packages are often made from recycled materials.

Activity:
Make New Earth Friends

1. Together with classmates and adults, ask the grocery store manager if you can borrow some paper bags.

2. Decorate the bags with ways to be an Earth friend.

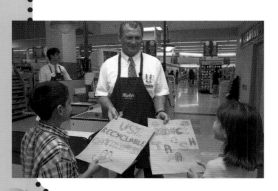

3. Return the bags to the grocery store so other customers will see how to be an Earth friend.